A TEMPLAR BOOK

Produced by The Templar Company plc,
Pippbrook Mill, London Road, Dorking, Surrey RH4 1JE,
Great Britain.

First published in the USA in 1991 by
SMITHMARK Publishers, Inc., 112 Madison Avenue,
New York, New York 10016.
SMITHMARK books are available for bulk purchase for sales
promotion and premium use. For details write or
telephone the Manager of Special Sales. SMITHMARK
Publishers, Inc., 112 Madison Avenue,
New York, New York 10016 (212) 532-6600.

Designed by Philip Hargraves
Edited by Amanda Wood and Andy Charman
Color separations by Positive Colour Ltd, Maldon, Essex, Great Britain
Printed and bound in Malaysia

ISBN 0-8317-7161-5

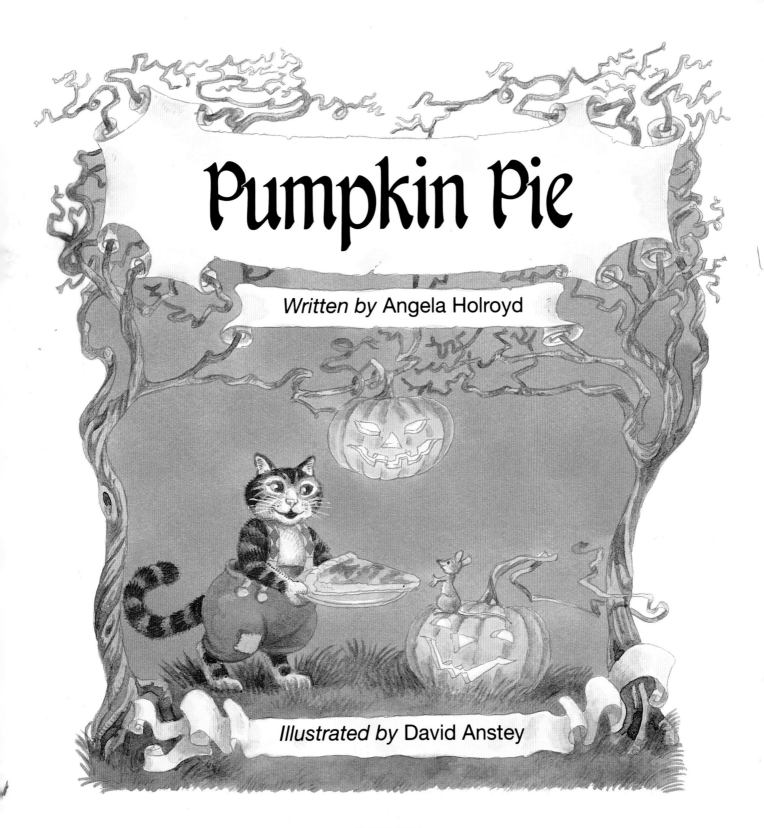

Pumpkin Pie

Written by *Angela Holroyd*

Illustrated by *David Anstey*

SMITHMARK

I t was Halloween, and all the animals in Catsville County were looking forward to the annual Halloween Ball that was to be held that night. As usual, Tabitha Tatler had made the pumpkin pie for which she was justly famous, only this year she had excelled herself. This time she had baked the biggest pumpkin pie that anyone had ever seen. It looked so tasty that her neighbors couldn't wait to get their teeth into it, and it was so gigantic that it had to be stored in Tabitha's backyard, protected from the wind and rain by a tent.

That morning, just after the wintry sun had peeped out to say hello, Tabitha bustled along to check the pie. There had been a fierce wind howling around the house the night before and she wanted to make sure that the pie was all right. But Tabitha was in for a shock. Instead of being perfectly round, the pie had a large, gaping hole in one side. And, what's more, it wasn't the wind that had caused it, for all around the hole there were teeth marks. That could only mean one thing – someone had been EATING Tabitha's precious pumpkin pie!

Tabitha Tatler was most upset, and before you could say "whiskers and tails" she had spread the dreadful news throughout Catsville. The Mayor of the town was furious – he always cut the first slice of pie at the start of every Halloween Ball. It was the grand opening to the celebrations, and now someone had actually had the nerve to bite a piece out of it! All through the day everyone gossiped about who could have done such a terrible thing – and the name on most of their lips was GREEDY GEORGE!

Now Greedy George was a very large tabby cat with a big, fat tummy and long, white whiskers. He lived right next door to Tabitha Tatler, and the thing he loved most in life was food. He could eat more ice-cream in one sitting than any other cat in the county and, when he was hungry, you could hear his tummy rumble on the other side of town.

About 6 o'clock that evening, George was returning home from skating with his cousins in the country when he came face to face with a group of his neighbors. They were huddled together under a street lamp whispering excitedly. As soon as they saw George coming, they stopped talking and looked the other way.

"Hello!" called out George merrily as he skated up to them. But not one of them answered him. "What time are we all meeting tonight?" George tried again.

"WE are all meeting at 8 o'clock," answered Perkins hotly. "But I shouldn't bother turning up if I were you."

"I'm surprised you've got the cheek to show your face, you greedy cat," added Tibby angrily.

George was baffled. He had not heard the news about the pie and was astonished when they told him – especially when they accused him of eating the missing piece.

"You needn't look so shocked," said Guss angrily. "After all it was you who pinched the last slice of my birthday cake."

"And my box of chocolate mice!" chipped in Ginger.

"And ever since Tabitha put that pie in the garden you've been drooling over the fence at it," said Max. "Why, only yesterday you said you'd do anything for a big, fat slice covered in cream!"

"But it wasn't me. I didn't steal any of it," George wailed.

But none of the other cats would believe him. After all, he was the greediest animal that they knew.

"And if you know what's good for you, you won't turn up at the Ball tonight!" said Perkins nastily. "You've already had your piece of pumpkin pie – and you won't be getting any more!" And with that they walked off, leaving poor George all alone in the windy street.

Now, George was not a bad cat. In fact, underneath his blustery, sometimes thoughtless ways, he was really quite kindhearted. Why, only the week before he had rescued a tiny mouse who had fallen in the river and had let him move into a hollow log at the bottom of his garden. But, although he was kind, George was greedy. There was nothing he liked better than a plate piled high with food, and everyone knew it!

"They don't want me to go to the Ball," blurted George to Marty Mouse the minute he arrived home. "They think I stole the piece of pie. It's not fair."

Marty had already heard the rumors. To be truthful, it had even crossed his mind that George might be the culprit. But as he looked at his friend's miserable face, he knew that George was not to blame. He watched anxiously as

George sat down heavily in his armchair. Then suddenly there was a loud rumbling noise. It was George's tummy rumbling! George was hungry! He looked up at Marty with a glint in his eye.

"If no one's going to believe that I didn't eat that bloomin' pie," snarled George, "then I might as well eat some of it!" And he rushed out of the door, pulling on his costume as he went.

Poor Marty didn't want to see George in even more trouble. But how could he stop him?

Once outside, George adjusted the wings of his costume. As a finishing touch, he tied a few red and yellow feathers onto the e̶n̶ of his tail. No one would ever recognize h̶i̶ up as an enormous vulture – a b̶i̶ and fluffy collar.

"I'll show them!"
fence that separ
decided t̶o̶
back̶
be

No sooner had he entered the jungle of twisted branches and scratchy bushes, than the moon disappeared behind the inky ouds. But in the distance he could see a clearing and, in the

f it

nd there, inside the tent, was the

ver seen. He licked his lips

way to the side of

mering light

ake his

At the sound of the voice, George froze to the spot. He turned his head just as the voice rang out again. It was coming from the pumpkin lantern.

"I have come to give you a warning," it boomed. "I am here to tell you that you are making a terrible mistake. You did not take the first piece of pie, I know. But if you take the second, your friends will be right to call you Greedy George. Help me catch the real thief instead, and you will be a hero!"

Poor George did not know what to do. The pie looked so tasty, and his tummy felt so empty – but he didn't really like his friends thinking he was a bad cat. So he moved a little closer to the lantern and stammered,

"Wh-wh-what do I have to do, then?" But before the lantern could answer, a scrabbling, scratching sound came from a pile of leaves in the corner of the tent.

"Quick! Hide!" urged the spooky voice.

George did not need to be told twice. He dived under the table in a flash. To his amazement, a mean-looking face with glittering eyes popped out of a hole hidden by the leaves. With a twitch of whiskers and a sly look around the tent, a big, brown weasel slunk into view. Standing up on his two back legs, the weasel sniffed the pie and licked his lips.

"Pumpkin pie!" he exclaimed and was just about the take a bite when George grabbed his legs and knocked him off balance. Before you could even say "Jack O'Lantern", the weasel was pinned to the ground. He struggled and snapped, but it was no good – George was much stronger.

Tabitha heard all the noise and came hurrying down the path. "Here's your thief," said George gruffly, disguising his voice. "I just caught him trying to pinch a piece more pie."

17

"Well, bless my soul! If it's not Willy Weasel up to his old tricks again," said Tabitha. "I thought he'd been booted out of Catsville County a long time ago."

"It's off to the kitchen with you," she said, taking the weasel by the ear. "I've lots of pots and pans you can wash up. Then we'll see what Sergeant Sam wants to do with you."

With that, Tabitha marched Willy Weasel off to the kitchen. But when she came back to thank the stranger in the vulture's costume, he had vanished – all that remained was one red and yellow feather, lying on the grass.

George slipped away, glad that Tabitha had not recognized him.

He was not sure that he deserved to be a hero. After all, if it hadn't been for the Halloween spirit, he would have been the one eating the pie. He had not liked the greedy look in Willy Weasel's eye one little bit. And he hated the thought of looking like that himself. Feeling miserable, he was about to slink off home, when Perkins, Guss, and Ginger appeared around the corner.

18

They had just been trick or treating and their goody bags were full to the brim with sweets and chocolates.

"Happy Halloween!" they cried when they saw George in his vulture's costume.

"Have a chocolate," said Guss, offering up his goody bag.

"Why, thank you!" said George in his gruffest voice, and then he did something very strange. Instead of popping the chocolate straight into his mouth as usual, he put it in his pocket and rushed off in the opposite direction.

"Who was that?" asked Ginger.

"Someone who wasn't very hungry," answered Guss.

"Well whoever it was, it doesn't matter now, because it's time we went off to the town hall to see the pie being cut," said Perkins, "even if Greedy George has been there first!"

19

own at the town hall, hundreds of animals were streaming through the large wooden doors. Everyone in Catsville County had arrived for one of the biggest parties of the year. There were brightly colored costumes everywhere – witches, wizards, ghosts, and skeletons wherever you looked. The Mayor, dressed as a vampire, stood on a platform. Beside him stood Tabitha Tatler and in front of them was the pumpkin pie, complete with a gaping hole in its side. The Mayor began his speech.

"I would like to announce that tonight a mystery hero caught the Pumpkin Pie Thief, trying to steal a second piece of pie! It was none other than that rascal Willy Weasel, who is now in Sergeant Sam's care." A loud murmur swept through the crowd as everyone began talking at once.

"Well fancy that!"

"I thought he'd been run out of town long ago."

"What a nerve that fellow has!"

The Mayor held up his hands for silence, then continued.

"We would dearly like to reward the hero, but he has disappeared. All we know is that he was dressed up as a vulture, and he left this behind." He held up the red and yellow feather.

Everyone in the hall turned to look at their neighbor. There were two animals wearing vulture costumes, but neither had the right color tail feathers.

The End